Caillou®

Happy Easter!

Text: Mélanie Rudel-Tessier • Illustrations: Pierre Brignaud • Coloration: Suana Verelst

chouette

It's Easter!
Mommy, Daddy,
Caillou, and Rosie
are spending a few days
at Uncle Felix's farm.
Caillou is happy to see
his cousins Amanda
and Emilio.

Caillou is fascinated
by the newborn animals.
Uncle Felix puts a little
chick in his hands.
"He's really small," Caillou
whispers. "I'm afraid to hurt him."
"Don't worry, Caillou,
he won't break," Uncle Felix says.
"You can pat him gently."
Caillou thinks the chick
feels very soft.

The children are
decorating Easter eggs.
Caillou is careful
not to break them.
Oooh… it's hard,
Caillou thinks, as he
carefully paints an egg
with his brush.

"When is the Easter egg hunt?"
an impatient Caillou asks.
"Tomorrow morning,
after the Easter Bunny visits,"
Aunt Ana replies. "And if he's
as hungry as you children are,
he'll want to eat a few
carrots. Do you think you should
put some out for him?"
"Yes!" Emilio exclaims. "Let's
go leave some carrots
for the Easter Bunny."

Caillou and his cousins
are looking for the best place
to leave the carrots so
the Easter Bunny will be sure
to find them.
"Here!" Caillou shouts when
he sees an old tree stump.
"The Easter Bunny is going to be
so happy," says Amanda.

Finally, it's Easter morning!
The children are so excited
that they can't sit still.
They dress quickly
and run out into the yard.
The Easter egg hunt
is about to begin!

"The Easter Bunny
has eaten all the carrots!"
Amanda calls out.
"I bet he left us some eggs!"
exclaims Caillou.
"Come on, let's start looking,"
Daddy suggests.
"Yay!" they all shout at once.

The children search
everywhere—in the bushes,
behind the flowerpots,
and between the tulips.
"I found another one!"
Caillou shouts.
The basket is almost
full already.

Grandpa and Grandma
arrive to find
their grandchildren happily
counting their eggs.
"Looks like the Easter Bunny
was good to you!" Grandpa
says, laughing.
"What beautiful eggs!"
exclaims Grandma.

The whole family
has gathered around the table
for Easter dinner.
Grandpa tells the children
that when he was a child,
everybody dressed up
for the Easter Parade.
His story gives Amanda an idea.
"Can we play dress-up
after dinner?" she asks.

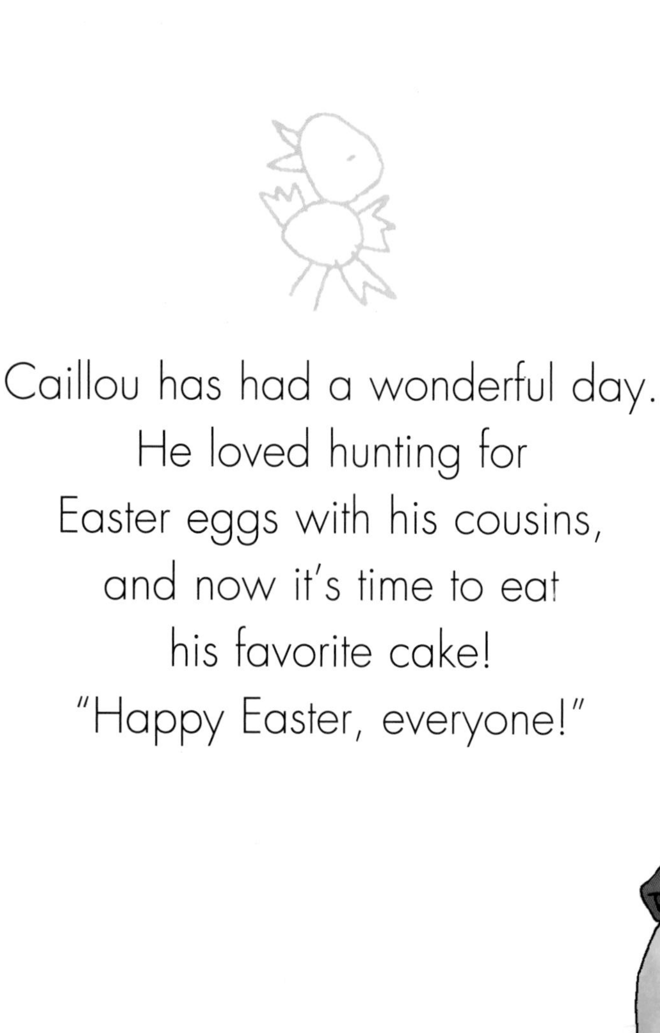

Caillou has had a wonderful day.
He loved hunting for
Easter eggs with his cousins,
and now it's time to eat
his favorite cake!
"Happy Easter, everyone!"

Text: Mélanie Rudel-Tessier
Illustrations: Pierre Brignaud
Coloration: Marcel Depratto
Art Director: Monique Dupras

We acknowledge the financial support of the Government of Canada through the Canada Book Fund for our publishing activities.

Canadian Heritage Patrimoine canadien

We acknowledge the support of the Ministry of Culture and Communications of Quebec and SODEC for the publication and promotion of this book.

SODEC Québec

Bibliothèque et Archives nationales du Québec and
Library and Archives Canada cataloguing in publication

Rudel-Tessier, Mélanie, 1975-
Caillou: Happy Easter!
(Confetti)
Translation of: Caillou: joyeuses Pâques!.
For children aged 2 and up.

ISBN 2-89450-386-5

1. Easter - Juvenile literature. 2. Easter egg hunts - Juvenile literature. I. Tipéo.
II. Title. III. Series.

GT4935.R8213 2003 j394.2667 C2002-941825-9

Legal deposit: 2003

Printed in Canada
10 9 8 7 6 5 4 3 2 1 CHO1822 JAN2012